Cowboy Grandma

COWBOY GRANDMA
Sarah King & Wendy Ault

NEW YORK

NASHVILLE • MELBOURNE • VANCOUVER

Cowboy Grandma

Published in New York, New York, by Morgan James Publishing. Morgan James is a trademark of Morgan James, LLC. www.MorganJamesPublishing.com

The Morgan James Speakers Group can bring authors to your live event. For more information or to book an event visit The Morgan James Speakers Group at www.TheMorganJamesSpeakersGroup.com.

ISBN 9781683505150 paperback
ISBN 9781683505181 casebound
ISBN 9781683501756 eBook
Library of Congress Control Number: 2017905045

Cover Design by:
Sarah King

Interior Design by:
Chris Treccani
www.3dogdesign.net

In an effort to support local communities, raise awareness and funds, Morgan James Publishing donates a percentage of all book sales for the life of each book to Habitat for Humanity Peninsula and Greater Williamsburg.

Get involved today! Visit
www.MorganJamesBuilds.com

Dedication

To our Tumbleweed and to all the adventures you will have—

never give up on your dreams

When Grandma was a little girl
she said she'd like to be,
"A cowboy! Yes! A cowboy, Mom!
A cowboy's life for me!"

"I want to roam the range and rope,
I want to wrestle cattle!
I'll ride a horse who likes to lope,
and never leave my saddle!

"A cowboy's life for me," she said,
"A cowboy's life for me!"

"Oh no!" Her parents said,
"Oh no! You cannot doctor cattle.
You'll grow up lady-like and cook,
And shake a baby rattle!
A cowboy you will never be,
a cowboy you won't be!"

Well Grandma was a rebel then,
and truly she was smart.
She doctored kids and ran a farm,
a cowboy in her heart.

She almost gave up on her dreams,
it seemed it was too late.
To learn to ride out on the range,
until our Mom said,
"Wait! Grandma you should learn
this stuff,
To ride and rope and play.
You aren't too old to have some fun,
a cowboy's life today!"

So Grandma rides and sometimes ropes,
she has a funny saddle.
She tackles every chance she gets,
to go and work some cattle!
"A cowboy's life for me!" She laughs,
"A cowboy's life for me!"

So when we visit Grandma now,
we never sleep in late.
There's no TV and no alarm
'Cause Grandma doesn't wait!
If Charles starts in crowing,
you'd best be out of bed.
So hustle all, down to the barn,
"Come on you sleepy-head!"

"We'll catch a calf and rope a cow, watch out for Bud the bull.
We'll go out early, come in late
summer's wonderful!"

And that was summer with our Gran,
no time to miss New York.
We rode and fed the chickens and
we learned to throw a rope.

And when the peep toads sang their songs
up in the big pasture,

We kids told stories all night long,
rapt in grandma's laughter.

"Don't give up your dreams my dears,
live life through and through!
Listen to those peep toads sing,
to yourselves be true!
What you choose to be is perfect,
be the very best you can.
Make a difference, do it singing,
think about your Gran!"

And when my Grandma got real old,
too old to feed the critters,
she moved herself up to New York,
and we thought she'd be bitter.
Instead she smiled and put her hands
gently on our faces,
"Some things," she said, "are better than
riding open spaces."

"I love you more than life itself,"
she said, "It's time for me to go.
Remember all the fun we've had,
I'll always love you so."

"A Grandma's life for me," she smiled,
"A Grandma's life for me."

About the Authors

Wendy Ault was born in California in 1950 and grew up totally passionate about horses, Roy Rogers, Gene Autry, and the Rose Bowl Parade—but only the horses! She noticed cowgirls were always waiting at home—not her Dream! She wanted to DO all the things cowboys do—ride and catch the cows, and chase the bad guys—and here we are. In between Wendy became a doctor, served in the Navy, fox-hunted, and rode a couple of tolerant horses regularly—working cattle any time she could get the chance. Somewhere along the line people stopped saying, "You can't do that, you're a girl." Wendy has been blessed with a wonderful daughter (a terrific horsewoman / artist) a great son in law AND a brand new grandson. She hopes he loves the horses as much as he loves the tractor!

Sarah King grew up in Virginia on a farm inside the Manassas Battlefield Park. Her mother always encouraged her to follow her passion and she became a multi-disciplinary artist and writer. Following her dream she moved to New York City with her husband, to pursue her MFA at the New York Studio School. She currently resides in Connecticut, where she paints, illustrates and teaches. She hopes to instill the lesson of Cowboy Grandma in her own son which is to never ever give up on your dreams.

Sarah would like to thank the members of the Morgan James Publishing team for helping her throughout this process, and for her friends Kamala Puligandla and Erin DeGiorgi who very patiently edited and re-edited the manuscript. She would also like to thank her husband for his never ending support, and her son, who gave her the inspiration to pursue this project. Lastly, she would like to thank her mother, who with a few, "I told you so's" and a lot of love and support, helped encouraged her to follow her own dreams. This is her second book. For more information on her art, or first book, The Great Adventures of Piggy, check out her website at Sarahakingart.com.

CPSIA information can be obtained
at www.ICGtesting.com
Printed in the USA
JSHW041745250123
36817JS00006B/27